To my brother, Ben
D. M.

For John F.
S. M.

First published 1998 by Walker Books Ltd
87 Vauxhall Walk, London SE11 5HJ

2 4 6 8 10 9 7 5 3 1

Text © 1998 David Martin
Illustrations © 1998 Susan Meddaugh

This book has been typeset in Stone Informal.

Printed in Belgium

British Library Cataloguing in Publication Data
A catalogue record for this book is
available from the British Library.

ISBN 0-7445-5610-4

Five Little Piggies

Stories by David Martin

illustrated by Susan Meddaugh

WALKER BOOKS
AND SUBSIDIARIES
LONDON • BOSTON • SYDNEY

This Little Piggy
Went to Market

"Little Piggy, will you go to market? We need eggs and milk and apples," said Mamma Piggy.

"OK," said Little Piggy. And she went to market singing,

"Eggs and milk and apples.
Megs and milk and mapples.
Pegs and pilk and papples."

When she got to the market she said,

On the way home she saw some chickens and cows
eating apples.

"Oh, now I remember!" said Little Piggy, and she ran
back to the market and bought eggs and milk and apples.

"Mummy, I'm back," said Little Piggy.

"Good. Did you get everything?" said Mamma Piggy.

"Oh, they're delicious pooples," said Mamma Piggy.
"And here's a great big **BUG** for my silly piggy wiggy."

This Little Piggy
Stayed at Home

SPLASH!

Little Piggy spilled his juice.

CRASH!

He dropped his cereal on the floor.

RIP!

His trousers split and
all the other little
piggies laughed
at him.

Mamma Piggy said, "I think you should stay at home with me today." And she sent the others off to school.

All day long Little Piggy and Mamma Piggy cooked and ate and played together.

"We had slopcakes and syrup for lunch!" said Little Piggy when the others came home from school.

The next day, all the other little piggies spilled their juice and dropped their cereal on the floor.

"Mummy, can we stay at home with you today?" they asked.
"Of course you can," said Mamma Piggy.

"Not me," said Little Piggy.
"I'm going to school."

This Little Piggy
Had Roast Beef

"Little piggies, come and eat," called Mamma Piggy.

"Not slops again!" said Little Piggy. "Why can't we have roast beef?"

"OK," said Mamma Piggy.
"Here's some roast beef."

"It's good, but
something is missing,"
said Little Piggy.

"Try some potatoes with it,"
said Mamma Piggy.

"It still isn't right," said Little Piggy.

"Here, dump in these bananas your brother sat on," said Mamma Piggy.

"Oh, that's good," said Little Piggy. "Can we put in the rotten eggs from breakfast, too?"

"Yummy!" said Little Piggy, and she threw in last week's soup and a squishy aubergine.

"Now it's perfect. Try some, Mummy!"

"Delicious!" said Mamma Piggy.

"But it tastes like slops to me."

"No," said Little Piggy.

"That's not slops. That's

ROAST BEEF!"

I want roast beef, too!

Me too! Me too!

This Little Piggy
Had None

One day Mamma Piggy went shopping and came home with treats for everyone.

But Little Piggy
dropped his
ice-cream

and his
balloons
flew away

and then Little Piggy
had none.

Little Piggy cried and cried.

"MUMMY!
I want
ice-Cream!
I want
balloons!"

Suddenly the other little piggies began to cry, too. And they cried even harder.

"Uh, oh. You four piggies all have chicken-pox," said Mamma Piggy. "But not you, Little Piggy. You haven't got any spots, NONE!"

"**Mummy! I WANT spots!**" said Little Piggy.

"Okay," said Mamma Piggy. "You can have spots, too."

This Little Piggy Cried Wee Wee Wee All the Way Home

Little Piggy was playing with the piggies next door.

Suddenly she got up and started running.
"Wee wee wee," she cried.

"Did you hurt yourself, Little Piggy?" asked Mamma Piggy.
But Little Piggy just ran faster and cried,
"Wee wee wee," all the way home.

Then she cried,
"Wee
wee
wee,"
all the
way up
the stairs.

And she cried, "Wee wee wee," all the way to the bathroom.

"OH!" said Little Piggy when she came out. "That feels better. I really had to go!"